Hi, there! It's your pal Hopsalot! Bebop and I are going to visit my family. Would you like to come with us? We are going to have a stupendous time. Don't forget to bring your pencil and some crayons for the super-fun games and activities we are going to do together.

See these carrot stickers? Each time you learn something new, you will get one to put in your picnic basket. When you finish a whole section, you will get a big flag sticker to add to your Certificate of Completion at the end of the book.

Here I am with my carrot. When you see this picture of me, it means I'm there to give you a little help. Just look for **Hopsalot's Hints**.

Ready? Look out, family, here we come!

Introduction

Hopsalot's Hints

There are words to read all around you. Do you recognize this **sign**?

EXIT

It shows where you can leave a building.

Bebop and I are on our way to visit my family! Help us get out of town. **Draw a line from each sign to the place it belongs.**

SCHOOL

STOP

LIBRARY

GROCERY

RESTAURANT

Post Office

Which shops have food? Circle the places where you can find a snack.

Oh, no! Bebop forgot his horn. We'll have to turn back. He won't go anywhere without music!
Draw a line from each instrument to its name. Look at the letters on each instrument for clues.

violin

horn

triangle

piano

drums

guitar

Sticker-ific! Place your carrot sticker in your picnic basket.

Word Building

We have to hop our way to Grandpa's house! My path is all the turtles that say **hop**. Bebop is using the turtles that say **step**. First, color in my path green. Then color in Bebop's path blue.

The words **step** and **hop** both have the same ending sound. Write it here:

Word Building • Kindergarten

Play a matching game with us. **Next to each picture, write the first letter in the word. Choose from the letters in the box. Then draw lines between the pictures that begin with the same sound.**

What do you think Grandpa might send to Grandma? Draw a box around it.

We're playing hockey with Grandma! **Draw a line from each stick to a puck that makes a word. There are some picture clues near the ice rink. Some sticks match more than one puck.**

__at

__am

__up

__oll

There are two toy words. Trace the words here:

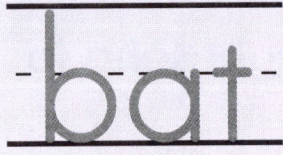
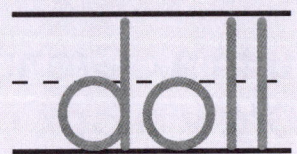

Grandma's pet polar bear cub messed up these words! Let's help them clean up the igloo. **Write the last letter missing from each word. Choose from the letters on the floor below.**

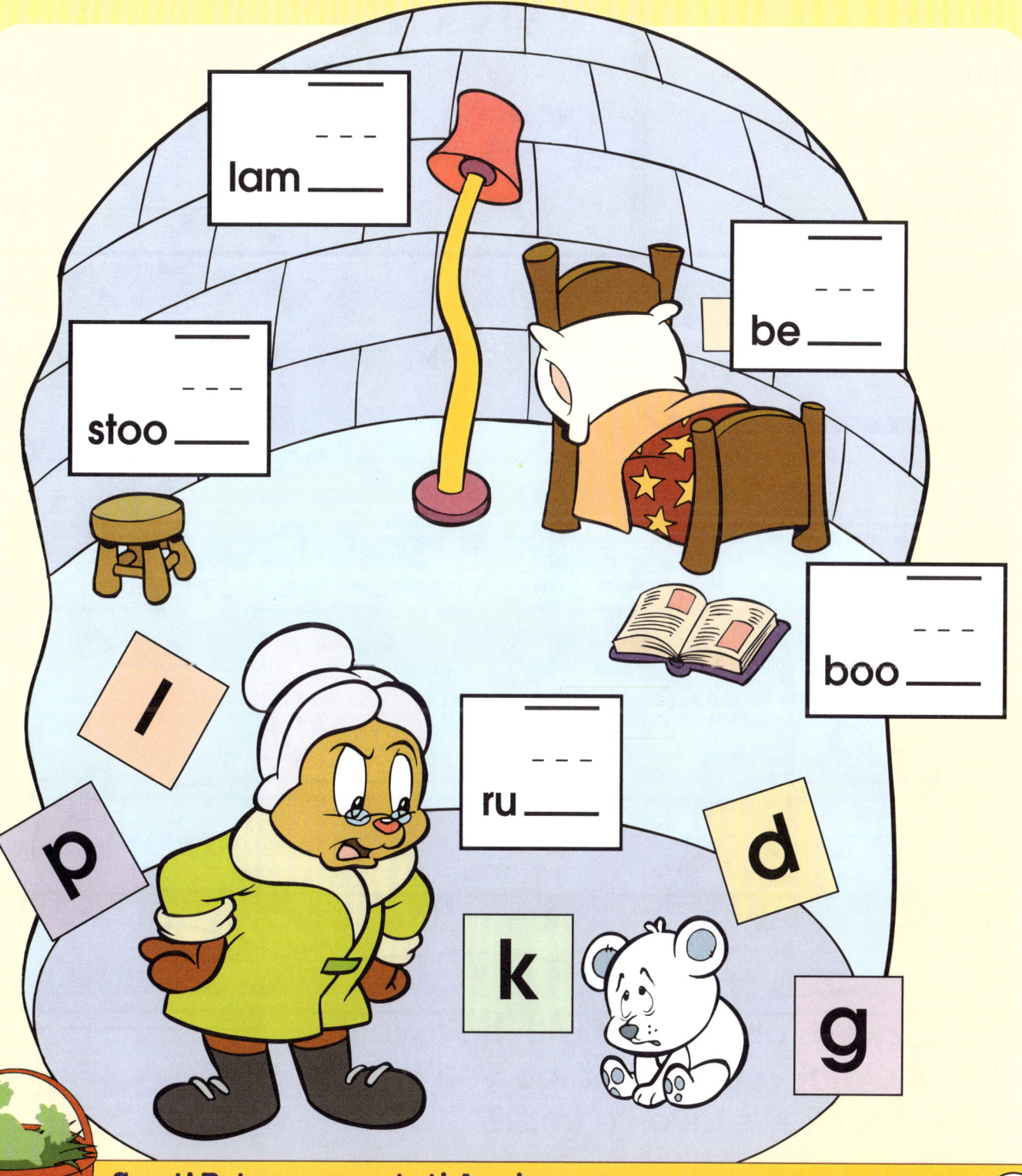

lam ___
stoo ___
be ___
boo ___
ru ___

l p d k g

Great! Put your carrot sticker in your basket and jump ahead to the next level.

Word Building

Hopsalot's Hints

Every word has a **vowel: a, e, i, o, u,** and sometimes **y.** Use these pictures to help you remember the **short vowel sounds:**

cat   ten   pin   top   nut

Flash's monkey friend, Crazylegs, ran off with the vowels! Can you help replace them? **Write the short vowel sounds from Crazylegs' sign in each word on the sand.**

a e i o u

f___x

s___nk

h___t

b___ll

Crazylegs also ran off with his favorite fruit. What vowel sound do you hear in the monkey's favorite treat?

Flash is going to teach Bebop and me how to surf! Cool! **Look at the pictures and unscramble the words on the surfboards. Write them on the lines.**

b O X   s ___   b ___   p ___   c ___

xob   nsu   lelb   nipk   trca

Surf-pendous job! Place your carrot sticker here and hop along.

Word Building 9

Level 3

Bebop is having such a good time visiting my family! To thank them, he wants to share one of his favorite games. **Color each space following the color key. The colors of the vowels will help you.** Now look for my initials (HB) hidden in the puzzle.

mop	top	job	lock
hut	cat	truck	fat
nut	mat	pump	dad
shut	hat	that	pat
duck	sat	lump	bat
luck	rat	cup	bag
will	pill	kid	sick

Review • Jump Start Kindergarten

Color Key
words with a = blue
words with e = green
words with i = red
words with o = yellow
words with u = orange

pot	hog	frog	not
ten	men	tub	bug
bed	gum	hen	jug
well	when	up	mud
shell	hum	red	hut
bell	pen	nut	drum
win	pin	kiss	sit

Very cool! You get your first big flag sticker! Put it on your Certificate of Completion. Now hop along!

Review 11

Hopsalot's Hints

Syllables are beats in a word. There are three **syllables** in my name.

Hops-a-lot
 1   2   3

Now we're on Uncle Romulus's farm! He always dances with his cows after milking time. **Say each word out loud. Color in all the boxes that have one-syllable words blue. Then color in all the other boxes yellow.**

- hay
- farm
- door
- dancing
- bucket
- Romulus
- cows

Treasure hunting is one of my favorite things to do on the farm. Romulus has hidden things for me to find. **Say each word out loud. Color in the word boxes that have one-syllable words yellow. Color in the other boxes red.**

Level 1

corn

wagon

dog

lamp

jug

frog

shovel

Stupendous syllable sighting! Put your carrot sticker in your basket and jump ahead.

Syllables 13

Let's drink hot cocoa in the igloo until the snowstorm stops. **Can you find three words inside Grandma's igloo that contain the word snow? Circle the pictures and finish the two-syllable words below.**

snow suit

snow_____

snow_____

We're syllable skating! Let's make some words. **Match up the syllables on the signs and trace and write the words on the lines below. The color of the signs will help you match them.**

igloo _____ _____ _____

Gracie will play with us after we find all the two-syllable words. **Say each word out loud. Then color in the boxes that have two-syllable words orange. Color in the other boxes yellow.**

Look at all the treats that were inside the piñata! **Say the picture name in each treat. If it has two syllables, color it in.**

balloon

squirrel

truck

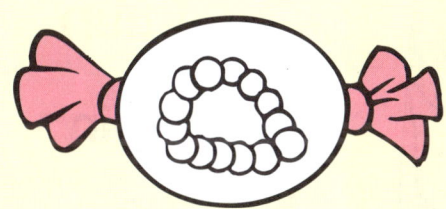
necklace

carrot

candies

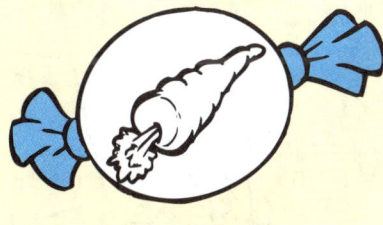
fan

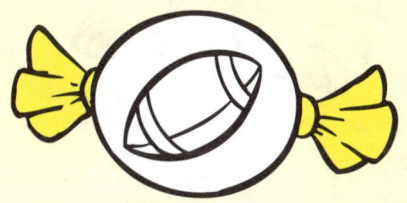
football

Great! Place your carrot sticker in your basket and jump ahead.

Syllables 17

Hopsalot's Hints

Words that are made up of two smaller words are called **compound words**.

cup + cake = cupcake

Flash has a compound word puzzle for us to solve. **Match up the same-color words on Crazylegs's cards to make compound words. Look for picture clues to help you.**

butter
cup
pin
cow

boy
wheel
cake
fly

Syllables • JumpStart Kindergarten

A giant wave smashed our canoes! **Help us to safety by finding the boat parts that go together.** Draw a line to match the boats that make two-syllable words. The colors of the boats and the picture clues below will help you.

- sand
- mer
- ham
- wich
- pump
- cil
- pen
- kin

Sea-pendous syllable saving! Place a carrot sticker in your basket and sail ahead.

Syllables

You can bebop with Bebop!

If Bebop is feeling sad and glum, you'll find him playing the big kettle ___drum___.

Bebop plays his saxophone when he hears the ring of the ___phone___.

At a square dance, in the middle, that's where Bebop plays the ___fiddle___.

Look at the pictures and read the rhymes. Trace the words on the lines and say them out loud. Then circle the ones with two syllables.

In the fields, he blows his horn. Farmers say it helps the _____ corn.

If it's piano you're learning to play, you should practice every _____ day.

Bebop is a superstar, playing music on his _____ guitar.

Nice job! Put your big flag sticker on your Certificate of Completion and jump ahead.

Hopsalot's Hints

A **sentence** is a complete thought. We begin sentences with a **capital** letter and end them with a **period**.

Grandpa likes to fish.

Grandpa gets lots of mail. Read each postcard and color the ones with complete sentences. Then add a period to finish the sentences.

Einstein

Einstein is an egret

an egret

green turtles

Einstein brings the mail

mailbox

snapping alligators

Grandpa likes to fish

The swamp is wet

22 Simple Punctuation • JumpStart Kindergarten

The bayou is a great place to fish! **Help us make complete sentences by drawing a line from the bait on our hooks to the fish below. Then add a period to finish each sentence.**

Fish-tastic! Put your carrot sticker in your basket and jump ahead.

Simple Punctuation

Hopsalot's Hints

A **question** is something that is asking for an answer! Look for this special **punctuation mark**:

We have so many questions for Romulus! **Trace these question marks by yourself and make some of your own.**

Now add a question mark at the end of each of our questions below.

What is this____

Is the plow new____

How does it work____

Where do you use it____

Romulus will answer all our questions.
Use the words on the barn to help us finish each question. The first letter on each line will give you a clue. Finish the word and write a question mark at the end.

Why do cows m _____

When does the rooster c _____

How high is the c _____

Who wants to fix the f _____

Simple Punctuation 25

Hopsalot's Hints

You can turn an **answer** into a **question** by putting the words in a different **order**.

Does Bebop need practice hitting the piñata? Gracie thinks so! **Use the words on each set of piñatas to trace each question. Put a question mark at the end of each sentence.**

Can he play?

Will it break

Is this fun

Can you help us get ready for Gracie's fiesta? **Find the word on the lanterns that finishes each question. Write it on the line below and add a question mark at the end. The first letter on each line and the pictures will help you.**

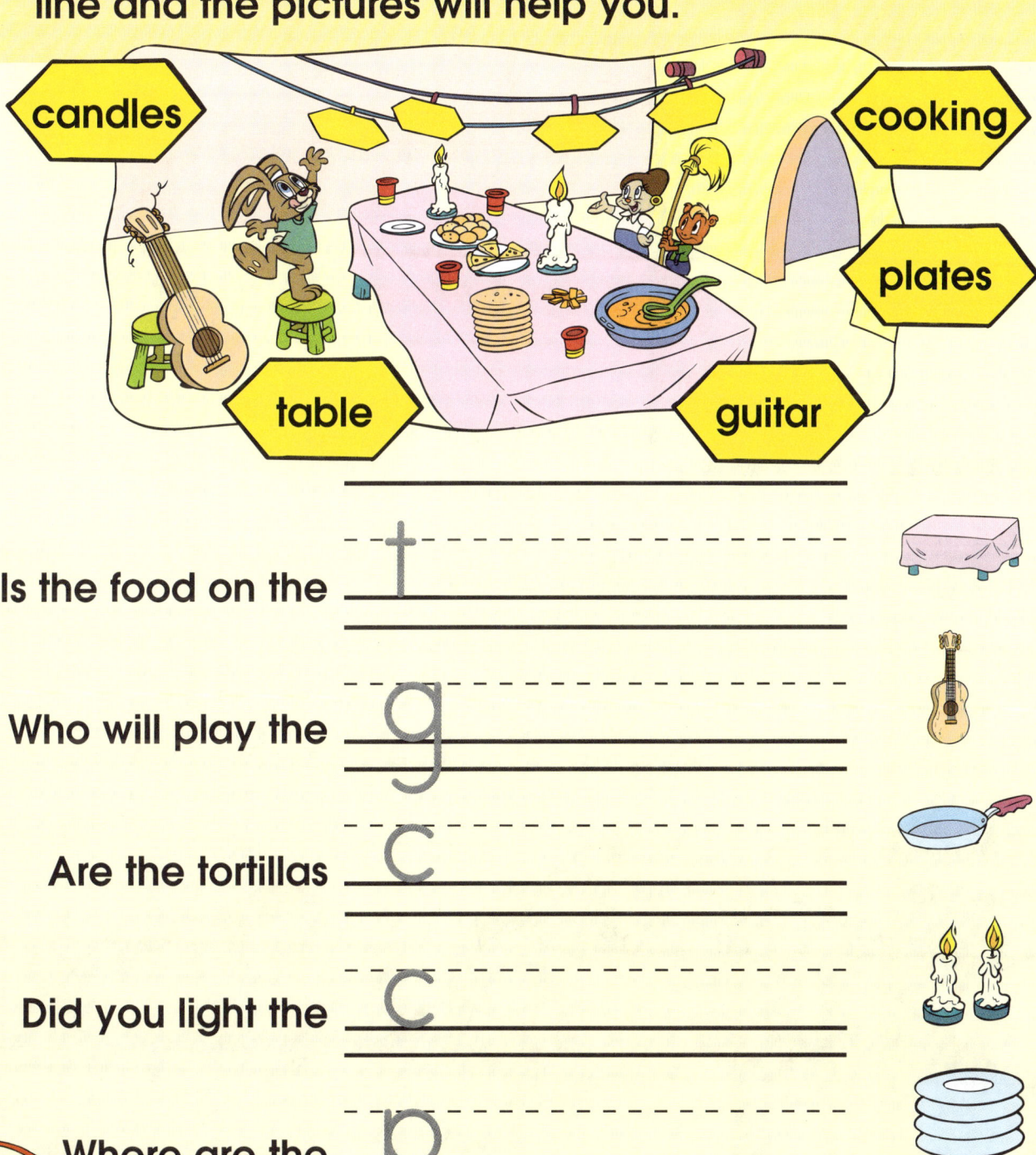

Is the food on the t_____

Who will play the g_____

Are the tortillas c_____

Did you light the c_____

Where are the p_____

Super! Put a carrot sticker in your basket and jump ahead.

Simple Punctuation 27

Hopsalot's Hints

This is an **exclamation point**: !

We use it instead of a period in sentences to show strong feelings.

Stop! That is too loud!

Let's go surfing with Flash! **First, practice tracing and then writing exclamation points on the lines.**

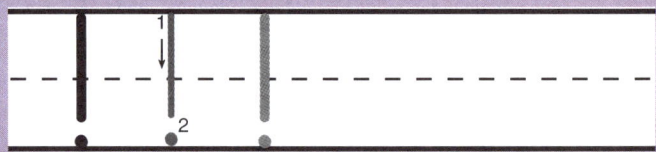

Then read the words on the palm leaves and trace each group to make a sentence. Add exclamation points.

Look at me!

The sand is hot

The water is cold

Let's race! **Trace exclamation points for the toucans so the race can begin. Then finish each sentence with the word in the box next to it. Add exclamation points at the end of each sentence.**

My _____ is fast

sailboat

I can surf on my _____

surfboard

I'll win the race in my _____

canoe

Excellent exclamations! Put your carrot sticker in your picnic basket and jump ahead!

Simple Punctuation

Bebop invited everyone to a party at his house. **First read the words on each space with a grown-up. Then add the missing punctuation:** . ? !

To play the game, you will need 6 pennies and a number cube. Put a penny on each character. Roll the number cube and look at the key to see how many spaces to move. Whoever reaches the party first wins.

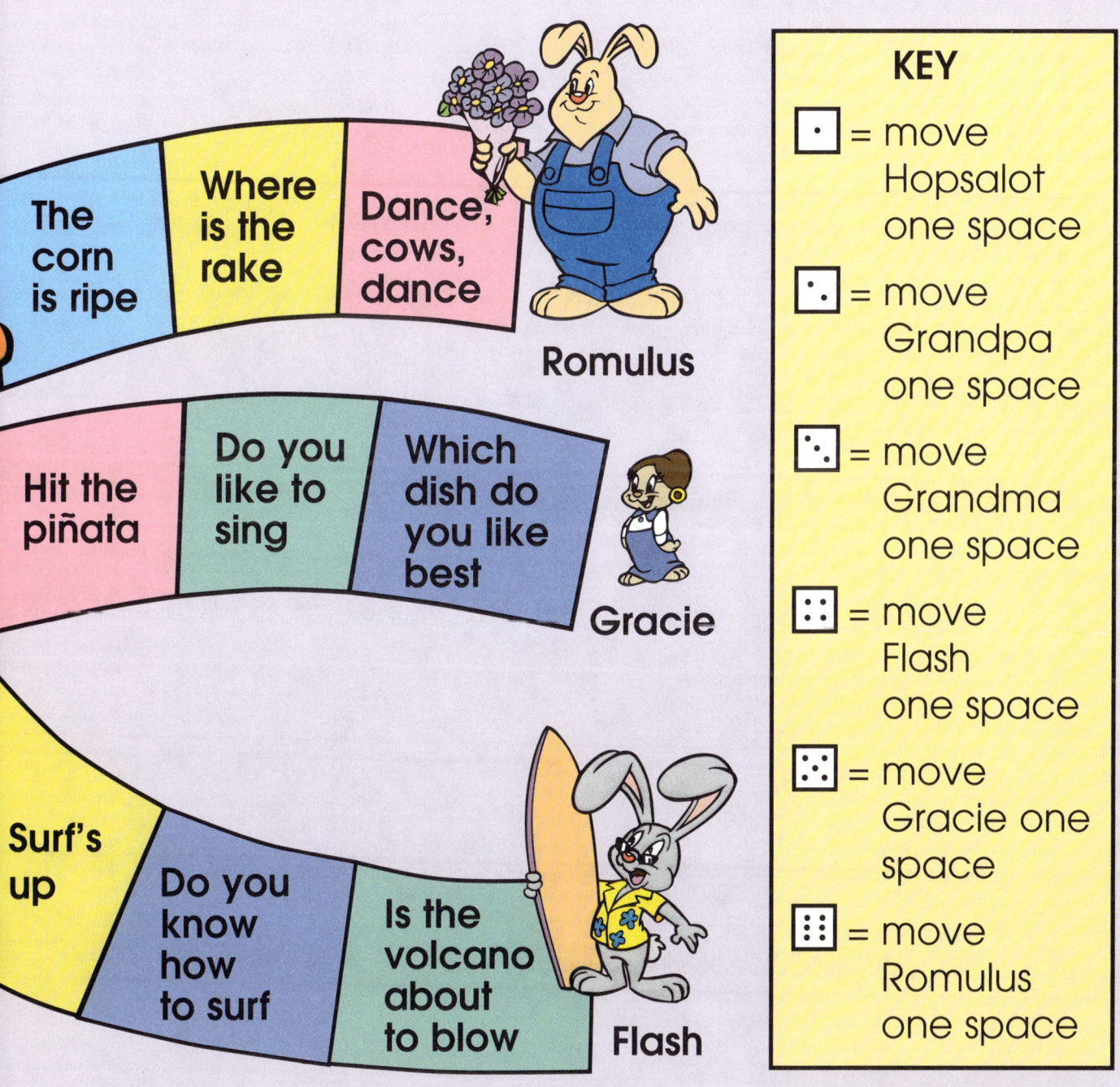

What a great party! Now put your last flag sticker on your Certificate of Completion! Great work!

Answer Key

PAGE 2	connect signs to post office, grocery, library, school, stop sign, restaurant; circle grocery store, restaurant
PAGE 3	connect Drums/drums, Piano/piano, Horn/horns, Violin/violins, Triangle/triangles, Guitar/guitar
PAGE 4	color five "hop" turtles green; three "step" turtles blue; write p
PAGE 5	write f, r, n, f, n, r; connect ruler/radio, nest/necklace; answers will vary
PAGE 6	connect j/am, b/at, c/at *or* up, d/am *or* oll; trace bat, doll
PAGE 7	write p for lamp, d for bed, l for stool, k for book, g for rug
PAGE 8	write a for hat, o for fox, i for sink, e for bell; a
PAGE 9	trace ox; write un, ell, ink, art
PAGES 10–11	mosaic reveals blue and green initials H and B
PAGE 12	color (blue) hay, farm, door, cows; color (yellow) dancing, bucket, Romulus
PAGE 13	color (yellow) corn, dog, lamp, jug, frog; color (red) shovel, wagon
PAGE 14	circle snowman, snowball, snowsuit, *or* snowflakes; trace suit; write man, ball, flake, *or* flakes
PAGE 15	trace igloo; write penguin, mitten
PAGE 16	color (orange) garden, seesaw, birdbath, turtle; color (yellow) tree, swings, wall
PAGE 17	color balloon, squirrel, necklace, carrot, candies, football
PAGE 18	connect butter/fly, cup/cake, pin/wheel, cow/boy
PAGE 19	connect sand/wich, ham/mer, pump/kin, pen/cil
PAGES 20–21	trace phone, drum, fiddle, corn, guitar, day; circle fiddle, guitar
PAGE 22	color and add periods to Einstein is an egret, Einstein brings the mail, Grandpa likes to fish, The swamp is wet
PAGE 23	connect The water/is warm, Grandpa/fishes every day, Alligators/have big teeth; add periods after day, warm, teeth
PAGE 24	practice writing question marks; add four question marks
PAGE 25	write oo?, row? orn?, ence?
PAGE 26	trace Can he play?, Will it break?, Is this fun?
PAGE 27	write able?, uitar?, ooking?, andles?, lates?
PAGE 28	practice writing exclamation points; trace Look at me!, The sand is hot!, The water is cold!
PAGE 29	trace three exclamation points; write sailboat, surfboard, canoe; add three exclamation points
PAGES 30–31	Hopsalot—Jumping gerbils(!) Can you come with us(?) It's fun to visit my family(. *or* !); Grandpa—Einstein brings the mail(.) Watch out for the alligators(!) Did you write a letter(?); Grandma—My igloo is made of ice(.) Will the penguins win the game(?) Go, team(!); Romulus—The corn is ripe(.) Where is the rake(?) Dance, cows, dance(!); Gracie—Hit the piñata(!) Do you like to sing(?) Which dish do you like best(?); Flash—Surf's up(!) Do you know how to surf(?) Is the volcano about to blow(?)